Mr Moo...
Aaaachoooo!

Sadie

Read more books in this series:

Mr Moo . . . I Want You

Mr Moo . . . What Shall We Do?

Mr Moo . . . I Love You Too

MR MOO . . . AAAACHOOOO!
A PICTURE CORGI BOOK 978 0 552 57607 9
Published in Great Britain by Picture Corgi,
an imprint of Random House Children's Publishers UK
A Random House Group Company
This edition published 2014

3 5 7 9 10 8 6 4 2

Copyright © Random House Children's Publishers UK, 2014
Illustrated by Julia Seal
The right of Julia Seal to be identified as the illustrator of this work has
been asserted in accordance with the Copyright, Designs and Patents Act 1988.
All rights reserved. No part of this publication may be reproduced, stored in a retrieval system, or transmitted
in any form or by any means, electronic, mechanical, photocopying, recording or otherwise, without the prior
permission of the publishers.
Picture Corgi Books are published by Random House Children's Publishers UK,
61–63 Uxbridge Road, London W5 5SA
www.randomhousechildrens.co.uk
www.randomhouse.co.uk
Addresses for companies within The Random House Group Limited can be found at:
www.randomhouse.co.uk/offices.htm
THE RANDOM HOUSE GROUP Limited Reg. No. 954009
A CIP catalogue record for this book is available from the British Library.
Printed in China

Mr Moo...
Aaaachoooo!

Illustrated by Julia Seal

Picture Corgi

One sunny Tuesday morning, Bella woke up feeling a bit funny. She was just about to say good morning to Mr Moo when all of a sudden . . .

Aaaaaachoooo!

"Bella, you're normally up and bouncing around by now," said Mum, but . . .

"Aaaaaachoooo!" said Bella.
Bella had the sneezes.

"Oh, Mr Moo," said Bella with a sniffle. "I don't feel well!"

Bella coughed and spluttered and sniffled and snuffled.
"No nursery for you today, Bella," said Mum.

Bella didn't want to stay at home.
"Perhaps I'm not so very ill," she said, but then . . .
"Aaaaaaaaaaaaaaaaachoooo!" Another huge sneeze
popped out.

"I won't have to go to the doctor, will I?" asked Bella through her snuffles.
Bella did not like going to the doctor.

"I don't think so," said Mum. "We'll just wrap you up warmly and give you lots of lemon, ginger and honey to drink – you'll be better before you know it."

"We'll have to find some fun things to do, won't we, Mr Moo," said Bella.
Bella curled up with Mr Moo and they looked at some of their favourite picture books together.

Bella was just about to settle down for a snooze when . . .
"Aaaaaaaaaachoooo!"
"Was that you, Mr Moo?" asked Bella.

"Mr Moo!" cried Bella. "You're poorly too!"

Bella got out
her doctor's kit.

She used the
thermometer.

She used the
stethoscope.

She even tried the arm–band–pumpy–thing, but
Mr Moo did not get better. In fact he looked more
and more unwell.

"Mum!" cried Bella. "We need to go to see the doctor."
"But you hate going to the doctor," said Mum.
"I've tried everything," said Bella. "But Mr Moo needs
a doctor . . . and I do too." And she did an extra big,

"Aaaaaaaaaaaachooooooo!"

"Well, you haven't had a check-up for a long time," said Mum. So she packed some of Bella's favourite biscuits into a little bag as a treat, and off they set for the doctor's surgery.

On the way to see the doctor, Bella felt nervous. She felt more and more nervous the closer they got. "Maybe I don't need to go to the doctor," Bella whispered. But Mr Moo did look very poorly.

In the waiting room, Bella felt so scared, she wanted to cry. She squeezed Mr Moo very tightly, and he didn't mind, even though he wasn't feeling very well.

"I want to go home, Mr Moo," sniffled Bella.

But when they finally saw the doctor, she was very kind. "You and Mr Moo will both be just fine," she said. "You need to get lots of rest and drink plenty of water. And perhaps have a little treat now and then." And she gave Bella a yellow lolly.

"Well done, Bella, you were very brave," said Mum
on the way home.

"Mr Moo was very brave too," said Bella as she sucked
her yellow lolly.
Mr Moo had a yummy biscuit too.

Bella and Mr Moo were poorly for two more days. Mum, Dad and Bella's big brother, Daniel, took it in turns to bring them soup on a tray.

On Friday morning, Bella woke up, and guess what –
she was feeling MUCH better!

Bella ran into her big brother Daniel's room.
"Daniel, Daniel!" she cried. "I'm better – look, I'm
better!" And she did a little 'I'm better' dance. But . . .

"Aaaaaaaaaaaaachoooooo!" said Daniel.
Now Daniel was poorly!

"I'd better get my doctor's kit out again,
Mr Moo," sighed Bella.

Mr Moo

Share this book with your child to help with:

• Language and speech skills
• Social and emotional development
• Key early learning concepts

Aaaachooo!
Bella is poorly - and Mr Moo is too.
But Bella is scared of going to the doctor -
can Mr Moo soothe her fears?

Also available:

Mr Moo...
I Love You Too

Mr Moo...
I Want You

Mr Moo...
What Shall We Do?

U.K. £5.99
ISBN 978-0-552-57607-9

9 780552 576079

www.penguin.co.uk

PICTURE CORGI